My dad THINKS he's funny

My dad THINKS he's funny

by Katrina Germein

illustrated by Tom Jellett

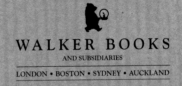

WALKER BOOKS

AND SUBSIDIARIES

LONDON · BOSTON · SYDNEY · AUCKLAND

My dad thinks he's funny.

Whenever I say,
"I'm hungry,"
Dad says,

"Hello,
Hungry.
Pleased
to meet
you."

Whenever I put lots
of sauce on my plate,

Dad says,

"Would
you like
some
dinner
with
that
sauce?"

the eye roll

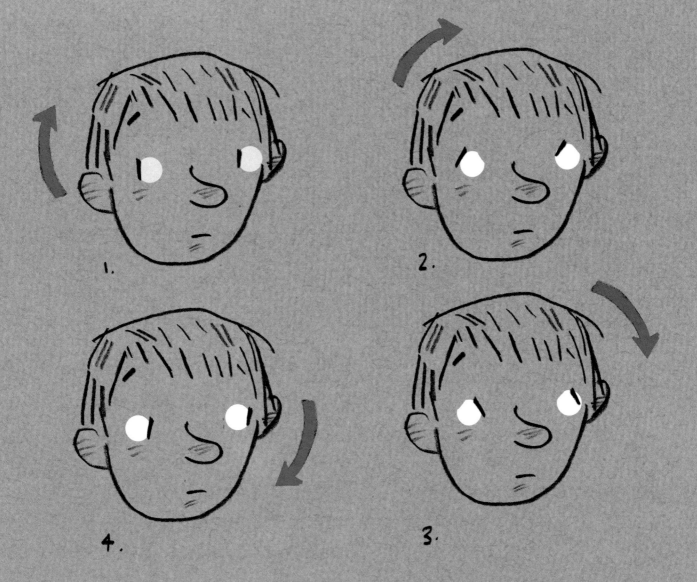

My dad thinks
he's funny.

When I say, "Dad, do
you know what?"
He says,
"I don't
know
What,
but I know
his brother."

When I say, "Dad, I don't
know how," he says,
"I know How — he's
What's brother."

And when I say, "Dad, I don't want to," he says,

"OK, then... Do you want three?"

My dad thinks he's funny.

When I tell Dad my finger hurts, he says,
"Let's chop it off!"

When I tell Dad my foot hurts, he says,
"No problem. You've got another."

And when I tell Dad I think there's something
in my eye, he says,
"Yeah, an eyeball."

My dad thinks he's funny.

If anyone asks,

"How's it going?" Dad says,

"By bus."

If I fall over, Dad says,
**"Welcome home.
How was your trip?"**

And if anyone asks,

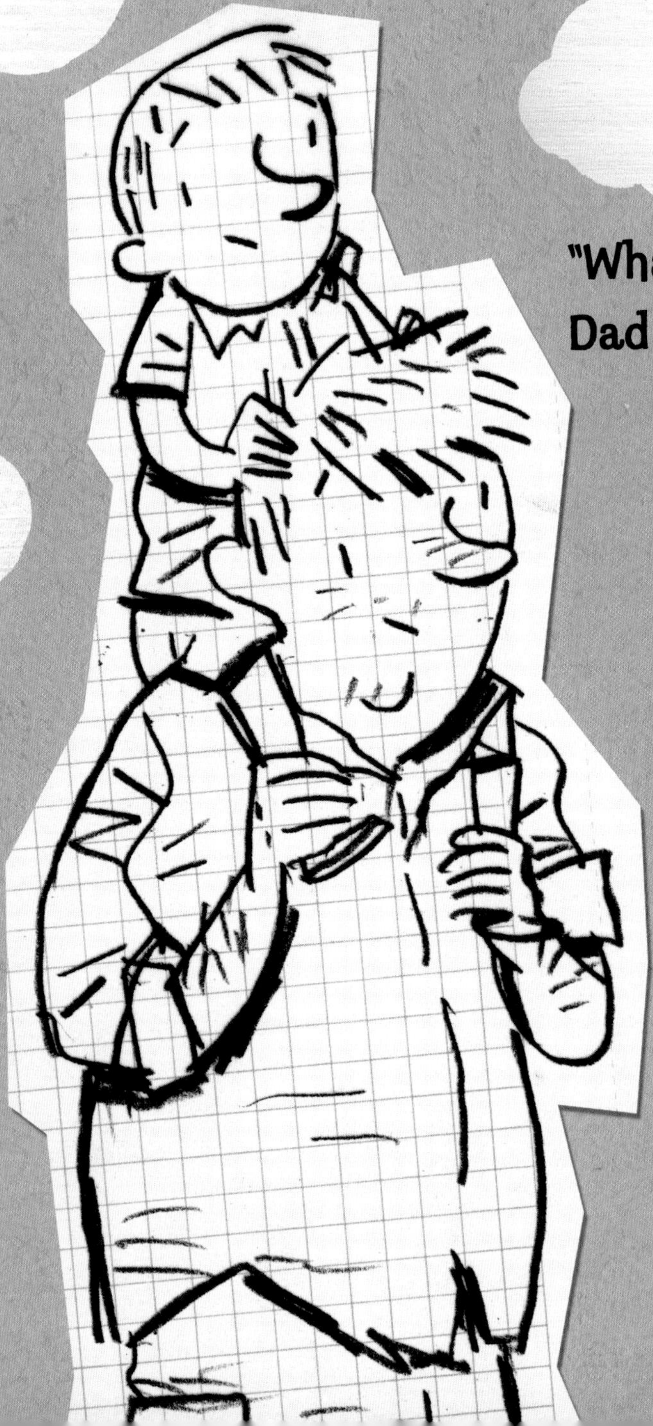

"What's up?" Dad says,

"Just the sky."

My dad thinks he's funny.

When people say,
"How are you feeling?"
Dad says,
"With my hands."

When people say,
"Would you like sugar?"

Dad says,
"I'm sweet enough."

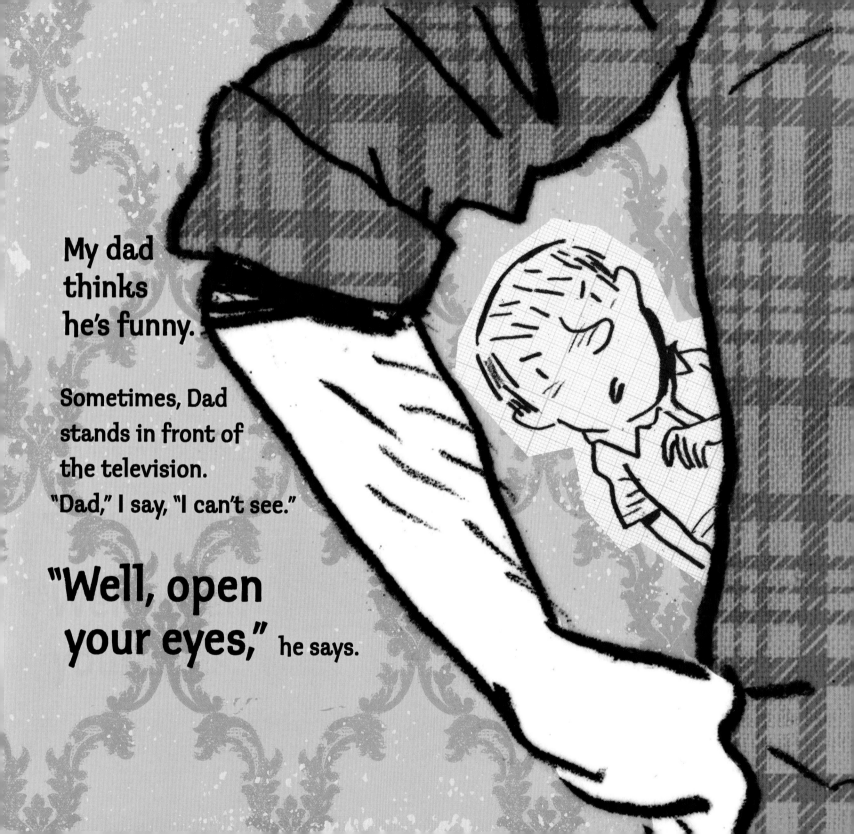

My dad
thinks
he's funny.

Sometimes, Dad
stands in front of
the television.
"Dad," I say, "I can't see."

**"Well, open
your eyes,"** he says.

My dad thinks he's funny.

Whenever I go swimming, Dad says,
"Try not to get wet!"

Whenever I go shopping, Dad says,
"Buy me some money!"

And whenever I go to
the toilet, Dad says,
"Don't get lost!"

My dad thinks he's funny.

When Mum says, "I'm just going to jump in the shower,"
Dad says, **"That sounds dangerous."**

And when Mum says,
"The neighbours' garden is
looking pretty,"

Dad says, **"Yeah, pretty strange."**

My dad thinks he's funny.

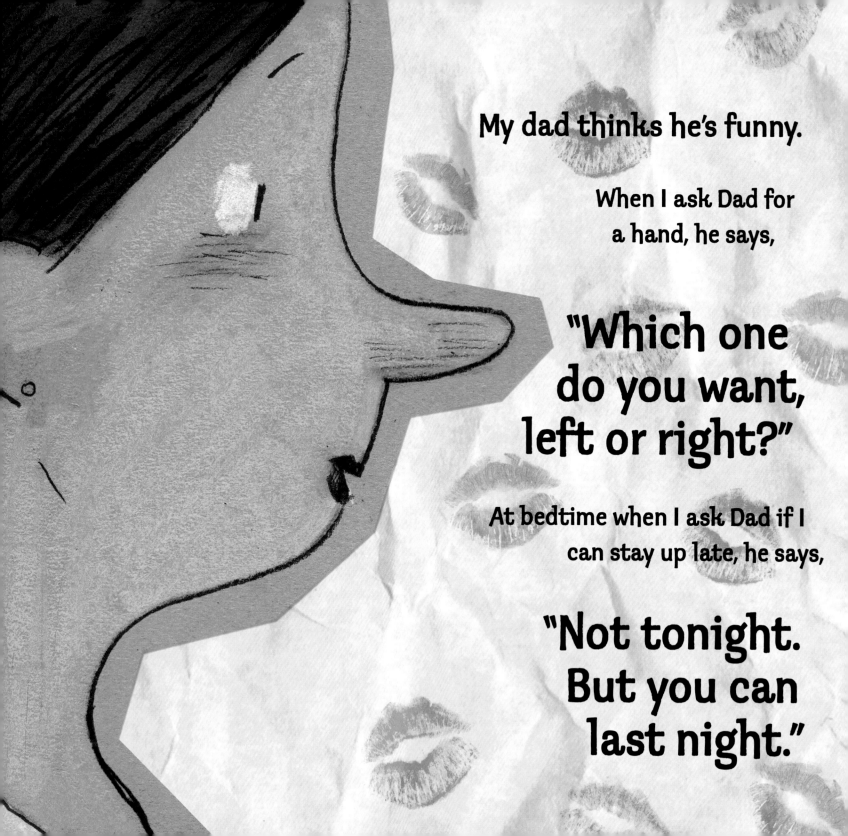

My dad thinks he's funny.

When I ask Dad for a hand, he says,

"Which one do you want, left or right?"

At bedtime when I ask Dad if I can stay up late, he says,

"Not tonight. But you can last night."

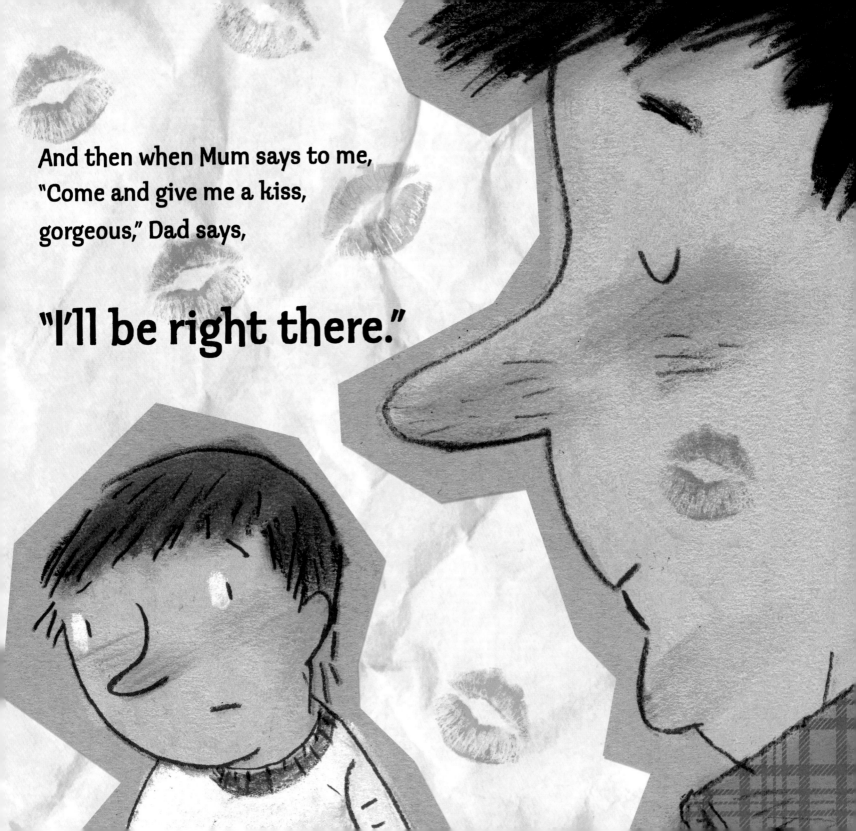

And then when Mum says to me,
"Come and give me a kiss,
gorgeous," Dad says,

"I'll be right there."

My dad thinks he's funny.

"Good night," I say when Dad
tucks me in.

"Good
morning,"
Dad says.

Then he pulls the
covers over my head,

kisses my feet

and turns on the light.

My dad
THINKS he's
funny!

For the dads — Grant, Honi, Steve and Alan, with lots of love. — KG

For Alfie, Charlie and Tian Tian. — TJ

First published 2010 by  black dog books

This edition published 2013 by Walker Books Ltd
87 Vauxhall Walk, London SE11 5HJ

10 9 8 7 6 5 4 3 2 1

Text © 2010 Katrina Germein
Illustrations © 2010 Tom Jellett

The right of Katrina Germein and Tom Jellett to be identified as author and illustrator respectively
of this work has been asserted by them in accordance with the Copyright, Designs and Patents Act 1988

This book has been typeset in Klepto ITC

Printed in China

British Library Cataloguing in Publication Data:
a catalogue record for this book is available from the British Library

ISBN 978-1-4063-4730-2

www.walker.co.uk